Disney's
My Very First Winnie

Pooh's Best Place

Adapted by
Barbara Gaines Winkelman

Illustrated by
Robbin Cuddy

SCHOLASTIC INC.

New York Toronto London Auckland Sydney
Mexico City New Delhi Hong Kong Buenos Aires

Published by Scholastic Inc., 90 Old Sherman Turnpike, Danbury, CT 06816
by arrangement with Disney Licensed Publishing.

SCHOLASTIC and associated logos are trademarks
and/or registered trademarks of Scholastic Inc.

ISBN 0-7172-8896-X

Printed in the U.S.A.

One afternoon, Piglet and Tigger were exploring in the Hundred-Acre Wood. They came upon some trees at the edge of a clearing.

"Tigger," cried Piglet, jumping up and down, "wouldn't this be the best place to play?"

"Yes indeedy!" shouted Tigger, bouncing up a nearby tree.

"No, Tigger," said Piglet, pointing, "in those birch trees over there."

"Sssay," said Gopher, popping up suddenly. "Did sssomeone sssay sssomething about a best place? I just found the best place to work!"

Rabbit, Pooh, and Eeyore had also heard Piglet calling. They all came running to see what was so exciting. Just as they arrived, Tigger—who was trying to bounce from branch to branch—tripped and tumbled out of the tree. CRASH! Everyone ended up in a heap!

As they began to untangle themselves, Piglet said breathlessly, "Come look at my new best place to play!"

"After that we can visit my best place for gardening," Rabbit said.

"Well, *my* best place," announced Tigger, "is everywhere! I can bounce everywhere because everywhere is the best place to bounce!"

"I have a best place for thistles . . ." Eeyore began.

"Oh, dear," Pooh sighed, sadly.

"What's wrong?" Eeyore asked. "Why do you look so sad?"

"Well, um," said Pooh. "I'm sad because everyone has a best place but me."

"You can use *our* best places, Pooh Boy!" exclaimed Tigger.

"Thank you, Tigger," said Pooh. "But I would really rather have my very own best place. Then I could share it with you, too."

"Come, Pooh," said Piglet. "Let's all go share our best places!"

"Yippee!" cried Tigger, bouncing down the path. "We'll have lotsa fun, you'll see!"

"I suppose I'll give it a try," mumbled Eeyore. "I might even have a little fun, too. Are you coming, Pooh?"

"Not just now," Pooh answered. "I do believe I'll go find my very own best place. Good-bye, everyone!" And he set off going the other way.

Pooh was so excited to find a best place that he didn't pay any attention to where he was going. He made up a song instead:

> Oh, my name is Pooh
> And I'll soon have a place
> That I . . . only I,
> Discovered by myself.
> Then it will be for everyone,
> A place to share and
> have some fun!

Suddenly Pooh saw a little pond in front of him with some stepping stones in the water.

"This could be a fun place!" thought Pooh. "I wonder where these go to?"

"One, two, three," counted Pooh out loud as he stepped on each stone, "four, fiiii—!"

Pooh landed in the water.

"Hmmm! It appears that last stone wasn't really a stone," chuckled Pooh. "It was a turtle. Silly me!"

Pooh looked around him. "Where am I, anyway?" he asked himself.

Suddenly he felt just a tiny bit scared. "And how do I get back home?" he wondered.

Pooh climbed out of the pond and walked on, looking for something that he might have seen before.

Pooh came to the entrance of a cave.

"Have I seen this cave before? We did play in a cave, once," he thought. "Maybe this is the same one?" He peered in.

"Helloooo!" called Pooh. "Anyone home?"

He was glad to hear a friendly voice answer him, "Helloooo! Anyone home?"

But then Pooh realized he was hearing his own voice coming back as an echo.

"Oh, bother!" he said.

"Oh, bother!" said the echo.

Pooh heard a fluttering sound. He turned around and saw many bats flying from the back of the cave.

"This is definitely the wrong cave!" said Pooh.

". . . definitely the wrong cave!" agreed the echo.

Pooh left the cave in a hurry and walked on. He was getting so worried about finding his way back home that he forgot all about looking for a best place.

On his way back toward the pond, Pooh saw a tree with a big hole. Inside was a mountain of acorns.

"Haycorns!" Pooh cried excitedly. "Piglet loves haycorns! Maybe this is Piglet's new best place?"

Pooh leaned in and called, "Hellooo?"

Nobody answered. But the mountain of acorns began to slide and tumble out of the hole. Pooh skidded on the little, round nuts and—PLOP! SPLASH!—fell down into the water again!

"Oh, double bother!" he said unhappily.

Suddenly Pooh noticed a familiar fence.

"I remember that fence!" he shouted with joy. "I walked beside it when I was singing. That must be the way to get back!"

Pooh was so happy to find his way, that he skipped all the way, singing:

> *Oh, I'd run a race*
>> *Just to see my friends!*
>> *My very best place*
>>> *Is with my Hundred-Acre friends.*
>>> *There's no better space*
>>> *Than with my dear,*
>>>> *dear friends,*
>>>> *Playing together all day!*

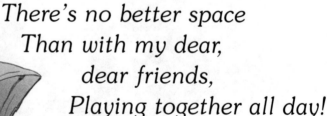

"Oh! There you are, Pooh," said Rabbit. "I was just about to organize a search party to find you."

"So," Rabbit went on, "did you discover a new best place of your very own?"

"Well, you see," Pooh answered, "at first I was very busy looking for a best place. But then I got too busy looking for the way home."

"Oh!" said Piglet. "So you didn't find any place?"

"Well," replied Pooh, "I did find four stepping stones and a turtle in a pond, a cave, and a tree-hole full of haycorns."

"A hole f-full of haycorns?" asked Piglet, his eyes shining.

"A cave? Tiggerific!" cried Tigger. "Let's go!"

"We can go . . . ," said Pooh, "but none of them is my best place."

"Don't tell me you found someplace you like even better?" said Rabbit.

"Where could that be, Pooh?" asked Piglet.

"Wherever my friends are!" proclaimed Pooh.

"Hoo-hoo-hoo! Me, too!" Tigger agreed.